THE BEATRIX POTTER COLLECTION
HILL TOP TALES

Four Original Peter Rabbit Stories

THE ORIGINAL AND AUTHORIZED EDITIONS

BY BEATRIX POTTER

New colour reproductions ™

F. WARNE & C°

FREDERICK WARNE
Published by the Penguin Group
27 Wrights Lane, London W8 5TZ, England
Viking Penguin Inc., 40 West 23rd Street, New York, New York 10010, USA
Penguin Books Australia Ltd, Ringwood, Victoria, Australia
Penguin Books Canada Ltd, 2801 John Street, Markham, Ontario, Canada L3R 1B4
Penguin Books (NZ) Ltd, 182–190 Wairau Road, Auckland 10, New Zealand

Penguin Books Ltd, Registered Offices: Harmondsworth, Middlesex, England

First published in this edition 1988

ISBN 0 7232 3548 1

Typeset, printed and bound in Great Britain by
William Clowes Limited, Beccles and London.

Contents

THE TALE OF
TOM KITTEN

ONCE upon a time there were three
little kittens, and their names were
Mittens, Tom Kitten, and Moppet.

They had dear little fur coats of
their own; and they tumbled about the
doorstep and played in the dust.

BUT one day their mother—Mrs. Tabitha Twitchit—expected friends to tea; so she fetched the kittens indoors, to wash and dress them, before the fine company arrived.

FIRST she scrubbed their faces (this one is Moppet).

THEN she brushed their fur (this one is Mittens).

T HEN she combed their tails and
whiskers (this is Tom Kitten).

Tom was very naughty, and he
scratched.

MRS. TABITHA dressed Moppet and Mittens in clean pinafores and tuckers; and then she took all sorts of elegant uncomfortable clothes out of a chest of drawers, in order to dress up her son Thomas.

TOM KITTEN was very fat, and
he had grown; several buttons
burst off. His mother sewed them on
again.

WHEN the three kittens were ready, Mrs. Tabitha unwisely turned them out into the garden, to be out of the way while she made hot buttered toast.

'Now keep your frocks clean, children! You must walk on your hind legs. Keep away from the dirty ash-pit, and from Sally Henny Penny, and from the pig-stye and the Puddle-Ducks.'

MOPPET and Mittens walked down the garden path unsteadily. Presently they trod upon their pinafores and fell on their noses.

When they stood up there were several green smears!

'LET us climb up the rockery, and sit on the garden wall,' said Moppet.

They turned their pinafores back to front, and went up with a skip and a jump; Moppet's white tucker fell down into the road.

T OM KITTEN was quite unable to jump when walking upon his hind legs in trousers. He came up the rockery by degrees, breaking the ferns, and shedding buttons right and left.

H E was all in pieces when he reached the top of the wall.

Moppet and Mittens tried to pull him together; his hat fell off, and the rest of his buttons burst.

WHILE they were in difficulties, there was a pit pat paddle pat! and the three Puddle-Ducks came along the hard high road, marching one behind the other and doing the goose step—pit pat paddle pat! pit pat waddle pat!

THEY stopped and stood in a row, and stared up at the kittens. They had very small eyes and looked surprised.

THEN the two duck-birds, Rebeccah and Jemima Puddle-Duck, picked up the hat and tucker and put them on.

MITTENS laughed so that she fell off the wall. Moppet and Tom descended after her; the pinafores and all the rest of Tom's clothes came off on the way down.

'Come! Mr. Drake Puddle-Duck,' said Moppet—'Come and help us to dress him! Come and button up Tom!'

Mr. DRAKE PUDDLE-DUCK advanced in a slow sideways manner, and picked up the various articles.

B^{UT} he put them on *himself!* They fitted him even worse than Tom Kitten.

'It's a very fine morning!' said Mr. Drake Puddle-Duck.

A ND he and Jemima and Rebeccah
Puddle-Duck set off up the road,
keeping step—pit pat, paddle pat! pit
pat, waddle pat!

THEN Tabitha Twitchit came down the garden and found her kittens on the wall with no clothes on.

SHE pulled them off the wall, smacked them, and took them back to the house.

'My friends will arrive in a minute, and you are not fit to be seen; I am affronted,' said Mrs. Tabitha Twitchit.

SHE sent them upstairs; and I am sorry to say she told her friends that they were in bed with the measles; which was not true.

QUITE the contrary; they were not in bed: *not* in the least.

Somehow there were very extraordinary noises over-head, which disturbed the dignity and repose of the tea party.

AND I think that some day I shall
have to make another, larger, book,
to tell you more about Tom Kitten!

AS for the Puddle-Ducks—they went into a pond.

The clothes all came off directly, because there were no buttons.

AND Mr. Drake Puddle-Duck, and Jemima and Rebeccah, have been looking for them ever since.

THE TALE OF
JEMIMA PUDDLE~DUCK

WHAT a funny sight it is to see a brood of ducklings with a hen! —Listen to the story of Jemima Puddle-duck, who was annoyed because the farmer's wife would not let her hatch her own eggs.

HER sister-in-law, Mrs. Rebeccah Puddle-duck, was perfectly willing to leave the hatching to some one else—' I have not the patience to sit on a nest for twenty-eight days; and no more have you, Jemima. You would let them go cold; you know you would!'

'I wish to hatch my own eggs; I will hatch them all by myself,' quacked Jemima Puddle-duck.

SHE tried to hide her eggs; but they were always found and carried off.

Jemima Puddle-duck became quite desperate. She determined to make a nest right away from the farm.

SHE set off on a fine spring afternoon along the cart-road that leads
over the hill.

She was wearing a shawl and a poke
bonnet.

W HEN she reached the top of the
hill, she saw a wood in the
distance.

She thought that it looked a safe
quiet spot.

JEMIMA PUDDLE-DUCK was not much in the habit of flying. She ran downhill a few yards flapping her shawl, and then she jumped off into the air.

SHE flew beautifully when she had got a good start.

She skimmed along over the tree-tops until she saw an open place in the middle of the wood, where the trees and brushwood had been cleared.

JEMIMA alighted rather heavily, and began to waddle about in search of a convenient dry nesting-place. She rather fancied a tree-stump amongst some tall fox-gloves.

But—seated upon the stump, she was startled to find an elegantly dressed gentleman reading a newspaper.

He had black prick ears and sandy coloured whiskers.

'Quack?' said Jemima Puddle-duck, with her head and her bonnet on one side—'Quack?'

THE gentleman raised his eyes above
his newspaper and looked curiously
at Jemima—

'Madam, have you lost your way?'
said he. He had a long bushy tail
which he was sitting upon, as the
stump was somewhat damp.

Jemima thought him mighty civil
and handsome. She explained that she
had not lost her way, but that she was
trying to find a convenient dry nesting-
place.

'AH! is that so? indeed!' said the
gentleman with sandy whiskers,
looking curiously at Jemima. He folded
up the newspaper, and put it in his
coat-tail pocket.

Jemima complained of the superflu-
ous hen.

'Indeed! how interesting! I wish I
could meet with that fowl. I would
teach it to mind its own business!'

'BUT as to a nest—there is no difficulty: I have a sackful of feathers in my wood-shed. No, my dear madam, you will be in nobody's way. You may sit there as long as you like,' said the bushy long-tailed gentleman.

He led the way to a very retired, dismal-looking house amongst the fox-gloves.

It was built of faggots and turf, and there were two broken pails, one on top of another, by way of a chimney.

'THIS is my summer residence; you would not find my earth—my winter house—so convenient,' said the hospitable gentleman.

There was a tumble-down shed at the back of the house, made of old soap-boxes. The gentleman opened the door, and showed Jemima in.

THE shed was almost quite full of
feathers—it was almost suffocating;
but it was comfortable and very soft.

Jemima Puddle-duck was rather surprised to find such a vast quantity of
feathers. But it was very comfortable;
and she made a nest without any
trouble at all.

WHEN she came out, the sandy
whiskered gentleman was sitting
on a log reading the newspaper—at
least he had it spread out, but he was
looking over the top of it.

He was so polite, that he seemed
almost sorry to let Jemima go home
for the night. He promised to take
great care of her nest until she came
back again next day.

He said he loved eggs and ducklings;
he should be proud to see a fine nestful
in his wood-shed.

JEMIMA PUDDLE-DUCK came every afternoon; she laid nine eggs in the nest. They were greeny white and very large. The foxy gentleman admired them immensely. He used to turn them over and count them when Jemima was not there.

At last Jemima told him that she intended to begin to sit next day— 'and I will bring a bag of corn with me, so that I need never leave my nest until the eggs are hatched. They might catch cold,' said the conscientious Jemima.

'MADAM, I beg you not to trouble
yourself with a bag; I will provide
oats. But before you commence your
tedious sitting, I intend to give you a
treat. Let us have a dinner-party all to
ourselves!

'May I ask you to bring up some
herbs from the farm-garden to make a
savoury omelette? Sage and thyme, and
mint and two onions, and some parsley.
I will provide lard for the stuff—lard
for the omelette,' said the hospitable
gentleman with sandy whiskers.

JEMIMA PUDDLE-DUCK was a simpleton: not even the mention of sage and onions made her suspicious.

She went round the farm-garden, nibbling off snippets of all the different sorts of herbs that are used for stuffing roast duck.

AND she waddled into the kitchen, and got two onions out of a basket.

The collie-dog Kep met her coming out, 'What are you doing with those onions? Where do you go every afternoon by yourself, Jemima Puddle-duck?'

Jemima was rather in awe of the collie; she told him the whole story.

The collie listened, with his wise head on one side; he grinned when she described the polite gentleman with sandy whiskers.

HE asked several questions about the wood, and about the exact position of the house and shed.

Then he went out, and trotted down the village. He went to look for two fox-hound puppies who were out at walk with the butcher.

JEMIMA PUDDLE-DUCK went up the cart-road for the last time, on a sunny afternoon. She was rather burdened with the bunches of herbs and two onions in a bag.

She flew over the wood, and alighted opposite the house of the bushy long-tailed gentleman.

HE was sitting on a log; he sniffed
the air, and kept glancing uneasily
round the wood. When Jemima
alighted he quite jumped.

'Come into the house as soon as you
have looked at your eggs. Give me the
herbs for the omelette. Be sharp!'

He was rather abrupt. Jemima
Puddle-duck had never heard him
speak like that.

She felt surprised, and uncomfortable.

WHILE she was inside she heard pattering feet round the back of the shed. Some one with a black nose sniffed at the bottom of the door, and then locked it.

Jemima became much alarmed.

A MOMENT afterwards there were most awful noises—barking, baying, growls and howls, squealing and groans.

And nothing more was ever seen of that foxy-whiskered gentleman.

PRESENTLY Kep opened the door of the shed, and let out Jemima Puddle-duck.

Unfortunately the puppies rushed in and gobbled up all the eggs before she could stop them.

He had a bite on his ear and both the puppies were limping.

J EMIMA PUDDLE-DUCK was escorted home in tears on account of those eggs.

SHE laid some more in June, and she was permitted to keep them herself: but only four of them hatched.

Jemima Puddle-duck said that it was because of her nerves; but she had always been a bad sitter.

THE TALE OF
SAMUEL WHISKERS
OR
THE ROLY-POLY PUDDING

ONCE upon a time there was an old cat, called Mrs. Tabitha Twitchit, who was an anxious parent. She used to lose her kittens continually, and whenever they were lost they were always in mischief!

On baking day she determined to shut them up in a cupboard.

She caught Moppet and Mittens, but she could not find Tom.

Mrs. Tabitha went up and down all

over the house, mewing for Tom Kitten. She looked in the pantry under the staircase, and she searched the best spare bedroom that was all covered up with dust sheets. She went right upstairs and looked into the attics, but she could not find him anywhere.

It was an old, old house, full of cupboards and passages. Some of the walls were four feet thick, and there used to be queer noises inside them, as if there might be a little secret staircase. Certainly there were odd little jagged doorways in the wainscot, and things disappeared at night—especially cheese and bacon.

Mrs. Tabitha became more and more distracted, and mewed dreadfully.

While their mother was searching the house, Moppet and Mittens had got into mischief.

The cupboard door was not locked, so they pushed it open and came out.

They went straight to the dough
which was set to rise in a pan before
the fire.

They patted it with their little soft
paws–'Shall we make dear little muf-
fins?' said Mittens to Moppet.

But just at that moment somebody
knocked at the front door, and Moppet
jumped into the flour barrel in a fright.

Mittens ran away to the dairy, and hid in an empty jar on the stone shelf where the milk pans stand.

The visitor was a neighbour, Mrs. Ribby; she had called to borrow some yeast.

Mrs. Tabitha came downstairs mewing dreadfully—'Come in, Cousin Ribby, come in, and sit ye down! I'm in sad trouble, Cousin Ribby,' said Tabitha, shedding tears. 'I've lost my dear son Thomas; I'm afraid the rats have got him.' She wiped her eyes with her apron.

'He's a bad kitten, Cousin Tabitha; he made a cat's cradle of my best

bonnet last time I came to tea. Where
have you looked for him?'

'All over the house! The rats are
too many for me. What a thing it is
to have an unruly family!' said Mrs.
Tabitha Twitchit.

'I'm not afraid of rats; I will help you to find him; and whip him too! What is all that soot in the fender?'

'The chimney wants sweeping—Oh, dear me, Cousin Ribby—now Moppet and Mittens are gone!'

'They have both got out of the cupboard!'

Ribby and Tabitha set to work to search the house thoroughly again. They poked under the beds with Ribby's umbrella, and they rummaged in cupboards. They even fetched a candle, and looked inside a clothes chest in one of the attics. They could not find

anything, but once they heard a door bang and somebody scuttered downstairs.

'Yes, it is infested with rats,' said Tabitha tearfully. 'I caught seven young ones out of one hole in the back kitchen, and we had them for dinner last Saturday. And once I saw the old father rat—an enormous old rat, Cousin Ribby. I was just going to jump upon him, when he showed his yellow teeth at me and whisked down the hole.'

'The rats get upon my nerves, Cousin Ribby,' said Tabitha.

Ribby and Tabitha searched and searched. They both heard a curious roly-poly noise under the attic floor. But there was nothing to be seen.

They returned to the kitchen. 'Here's one of your kittens at least,' said Ribby, dragging Moppet out of the flour barrel.

They shook the flour off her and set her down on the kitchen floor. She seemed to be in a terrible fright.

'Oh! Mother, Mother,' said Moppet, 'there's been an old woman rat in the kitchen, and she's stolen some of the dough!'

The two cats ran to look at the dough pan. Sure enough there were marks of little scratching fingers, and a lump of dough was gone!

'Which way did she go, Moppet?'

But Moppet had been too much frightened to peep out of the barrel again.

Ribby and Tabitha took her with them to keep her safely in sight, while they went on with their search.

They went into the dairy.

The first thing they found was Mittens, hiding in an empty jar.

They tipped up the jar, and she scrambled out.

'Oh, Mother, Mother!' said Mittens—

'Oh! Mother, Mother, there has been an old man rat in the dairy—a dreadful 'normous big rat, mother; and he's stolen a pat of butter and the rolling-pin.'

Ribby and Tabitha looked at one another.

'A rolling-pin and butter! Oh, my poor son Thomas!' exclaimed Tabitha, wringing her paws.

'A rolling-pin?' said Ribby. 'Did we not hear a roly-poly noise in the attic when we were looking into that chest?'

Ribby and Tabitha rushed upstairs again. Sure enough the roly-poly noise was still going on quite distinctly under the attic floor.

'This is serious, Cousin Tabitha,' said Ribby. 'We must send for John Joiner at once, with a saw.'

*　　*　　*　　*　　*

Now this is what had been happening to Tom Kitten, and it shows how very unwise it is to go up a chimney in a very old house, where a person does not know his way, and where there are enormous rats.

Tom Kitten did not want to be shut up in a cupboard. When he saw that his mother was going to bake, he determined to hide.

He looked about for a nice convenient place, and he fixed upon the chimney.

The fire had only just been lighted, and it was not hot; but there was a

white choky smoke from the green sticks. Tom Kitten got upon the fender and looked up. It was a big old-fashioned fire-place.

The chimney itself was wide enough inside for a man to stand up and walk about. So there was plenty of room for a little Tom Cat.

He jumped right up into the fire-place, balancing himself upon the iron bar where the kettle hangs.

Tom Kitten took another big jump

off the bar, and landed on a ledge
high up inside the chimney, knocking
down some soot into the fender.

Tom Kitten coughed and choked
with the smoke; and he could hear the
sticks beginning to crackle and burn
in the fire-place down below. He made
up his mind to climb right to the top,
and get out on the slates, and try to
catch sparrows.

'I cannot go back. If I slipped I
might fall in the fire and singe my
beautiful tail and my little blue jacket.'

The chimney was a very big old-fashioned one. It was built in the days when people burnt logs of wood upon the hearth.

The chimney stack stood up above the roof like a little stone tower, and the daylight shone down from the top, under the slanting slates that kept out the rain.

Tom Kitten was getting very frightened! He climbed up, and up, and up.

Then he waded sideways through inches of soot. He was like a little sweep himself.

It was most confusing in the dark. One flue seemed to lead into another.

There was less smoke, but Tom Kitten felt quite lost.

He scrambled up and up; but before he reached the chimney top he came to a place where somebody had loosened a stone in the wall. There were some mutton bones lying about—

'This seems funny,' said Tom Kitten. 'Who has been gnawing bones up here in the chimney? I wish I had never come! And what a funny smell? It is something like mouse; only dreadfully strong. It makes me sneeze,' said Tom Kitten.

He squeezed through the hole in the
wall, and dragged himself along a most
uncomfortably tight passage where
there was scarcely any light.

He groped his way carefully for
several yards; he was at the back of
the skirting-board in the attic, where
there is a little mark * in the picture.

All at once he fell head over heels in the dark, down a hole, and landed on a heap of very dirty rags.

When Tom Kitten picked himself up and looked about him—he found himself in a place that he had never seen before, although he had lived all his life in the house.

It was a very small stuffy fusty room, with boards, and rafters, and cobwebs, and lath and plaster.

Opposite to him—as far away as he could sit—was an enormous rat.

'What do you mean by tumbling into my bed all covered with smuts?' said the rat, chattering his teeth.

'Please sir, the chimney wants sweeping,' said poor Tom Kitten.

'Anna Maria! Anna Maria!' squeaked the rat. There was a pattering noise and an old woman rat poked her head round a rafter.

All in a minute she rushed upon
Tom Kitten, and before he knew what
was happening—

His coat was pulled off, and he was
rolled up in a bundle, and tied with
string in very hard knots.

Anna Maria did the tying. The old
rat watched her and took snuff. When
she had finished, they both sat staring
at him with their mouths open.

'Anna Maria,' said the old man rat (whose name was Samuel Whiskers),— 'Anna Maria, make me a kitten dumpling roly-poly pudding for my dinner.'

'It requires dough and a pat of butter, and a rolling-pin,' said Anna Maria, considering Tom Kitten with her head on one side.

'No,' said Samuel Whiskers, 'make it properly, Anna Maria, with bread-crumbs.'

'Nonsense! Butter and dough,' replied Anna Maria.

The two rats consulted together for a few minutes and then went away. Samuel Whiskers got through a

hole in the wainscot, and went boldly down the front staircase to the dairy to get the butter. He did not meet anybody.

He made a second journey for the rolling-pin. He pushed it in front of him with his paws, like a brewer's man trundling a barrel.

He could hear Ribby and Tabitha talking, but they were busy lighting the candle to look into the chest.

They did not see him.

Anna Maria went down by way of the skirting-board and a window shutter to the kitchen to steal the dough.

She borrowed a small saucer, and scooped up the dough with her paws.

She did not observe Moppet.

While Tom Kitten was left alone under the floor of the attic, he wriggled about and tried to mew for help.

But his mouth was full of soot and cobwebs, and he was tied up in such very tight knots, he could not make anybody hear him.

Except a spider, which came out of a crack in the ceiling and examined the knots critically, from a safe distance.

It was a judge of knots because it had a habit of tying up unfortunate blue-bottles. It did not offer to assist him.

Tom Kitten wriggled and squirmed until he was quite exhausted.

Presently the rats came back and set to work to make him into a dumpling. First they smeared him with butter, and then they rolled him in the dough.

'Will not the string be very indigestible, Anna Maria?' inquired Samuel Whiskers.

Anna Maria said she thought that it was of no consequence; but she wished that Tom Kitten would hold his head still, as it disarranged the pastry. She laid hold of his ears.

Tom Kitten bit and spat, and mewed and wriggled; and the rolling-pin went roly-poly, roly; roly, poly, roly. The rats each held an end.

'His tail is sticking out! You did not fetch enough dough, Anna Maria.'

'I fetched as much as I could carry,' replied Anna Maria.

'I do not think'—said Samuel Whiskers, pausing to take a look at Tom Kitten—'I do *not* think it will be a good pudding. It smells sooty.'

Anna Maria was about to argue the point, when all at once there began to be other sounds up above—the rasping noise of a saw; and the noise of a little dog, scratching and yelping!

The rats dropped the rolling-pin, and listened attentively.

'We are discovered and interrupted, Anna Maria; let us collect our property—and other people's,—and depart at once.'

'I fear that we shall be obliged to leave this pudding.'

'But I am persuaded that the knots would have proved indigestible, whatever you may urge to the contrary.'

'Come away at once and help me to tie up some mutton bones in a counterpane,' said Anna Maria. 'I have got half a smoked ham hidden in the chimney.'

So it happened that by the time
John Joiner had got the plank up—
there was nobody under the floor
except the rolling-pin and Tom Kitten
in a very dirty dumpling!

But there was a strong smell of rats; and John Joiner spent the rest of the morning sniffing and whining, and wagging his tail, and going round and round with his head in the hole like a gimlet.

Then he nailed the plank down again and put his tools in his bag, and came downstairs.

The cat family had quite recovered. They invited him to stay to dinner.

The dumpling had been peeled off Tom Kitten, and made separately into a bag pudding, with currants in it to hide the smuts.

They had been obliged to put Tom Kitten into a hot bath to get the butter off.

John Joiner smelt the pudding; but
he regretted that he had not time to
stay to dinner, because he had just
finished making a wheel-barrow for
Miss Potter, and she had ordered two
hen-coops.

And when I was going to the post
late in the afternoon—I looked up the
lane from the corner, and I saw Mr.
Samuel Whiskers and his wife on the

run, with big bundles on a little wheel-
barrow, which looked very like mine.

They were just turning in at the
gate to the barn of Farmer Potatoes.

Samuel Whiskers was puffing and
out of breath. Anna Maria was still
arguing in shrill tones.

She seemed to know her way, and
she seemed to have a quantity of
luggage.

I am sure *I* never gave her leave to
borrow my wheel-barrow!

They went into the barn, and hauled
their parcels with a bit of string to the
top of the hay mow.

After that, there were no more rats for a long time at Tabitha Twitchit's.

As for Farmer Potatoes, he has been driven nearly distracted. There are rats, and rats, and rats in his barn! They eat up the chicken food, and steal the oats and bran, and make holes in the meal bags.

And they are all descended from Mr. and Mrs. Samuel Whiskers—children and grand-children and great great grand-children.

There is no end to them!

Moppet and Mittens have grown up into very good rat-catchers.

They go out rat-catching in the village, and they find plenty of employment. They charge so much a dozen, and earn their living very comfortably.

They hang up the rats' tails in a
row on the barn door, to show how
many they have caught—dozens and
dozens of them.

But Tom Kitten has always been
afraid of a rat; he never durst face
anything that is bigger than—

A Mouse.

THE TALE OF
GINGER AND PICKLES

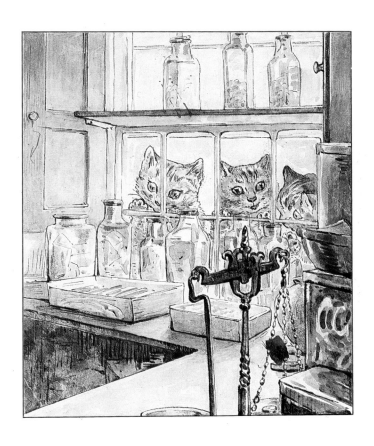

ONCE upon a time there was a village shop. The name over the window was 'Ginger and Pickles.'

It was a little small shop just the right size for Dolls—Lucinda and Jane Doll-cook always bought their groceries at Ginger and Pickles.

The counter inside was a convenient height for rabbits. Ginger and Pickles sold red spotty pocket-handkerchiefs at a penny three farthings.

They also sold sugar, and snuff and galoshes.

In fact, although it was such a small shop it sold nearly everything—except a few things that you want in a hurry—like bootlaces, hair-pins and mutton chops.

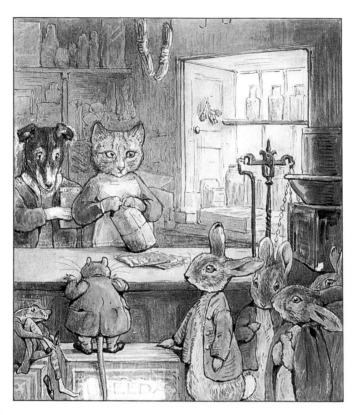

Ginger and Pickles were the people who kept the shop. Ginger was a yellow tom-cat, and Pickles was a terrier.

The rabbits were always a little bit afraid of Pickles.

The shop was also patronized by mice—only the mice were rather afraid of Ginger.

Ginger usually requested Pickles to serve them, because he said it made his mouth water.

'I cannot bear,' said he, 'to see them going out at the door carrying their little parcels.'

'I have the same feeling about rats,' replied Pickles, 'but it would never do to eat our own customers; they would leave us and go to Tabitha Twitchit's.'

'On the contrary, they would go nowhere,' replied Ginger gloomily.

(Tabitha Twitchit kept the only other shop in the village. She did not give credit.)

Ginger and Pickles gave unlimited credit.

Now the meaning of 'credit' is this—when a customer buys a bar of soap, instead of the customer pulling out a purse and paying for it—she says she will pay another time.

And Pickles makes a low bow and says, 'With pleasure, madam,' and it is written down in a book.

The customers come again and again, and buy quantities, in spite of being afraid of Ginger and Pickles.

But there is no money in what is called the 'till.'

The customers came in crowds every
day and bought quantities, especially
the toffee customers. But there was
always no money; they never paid for
as much as a pennyworth of pepper-
mints.

But the sales were enormous, ten
times as large as Tabitha Twitchit's.

As there was always no money, Ginger and Pickles were obliged to eat their own goods.

Pickles ate biscuits and Ginger ate a dried haddock.

They ate them by candle-light after the shop was closed.

When it came to Jan. 1st there was still no money, and Pickles was unable to buy a dog licence.

'It is very unpleasant, I am afraid of the police,' said Pickles.

'It is your own fault for being a

terrier; *I* do not require a licence, and
neither does Kep, the Collie dog.'

'It is very uncomfortable, I am afraid
I shall be summoned. I have tried in
vain to get a licence upon credit at the
Post Office;' said Pickles. 'The place
is full of policemen. I met one as I
was coming home.'

'Let us send in the bill again to Samuel Whiskers, Ginger, he owes 22/9 for bacon.'

'I do not believe that he intends to pay at all,' replied Ginger.

'And I feel sure that Anna Maria pockets things—Where are all the cream crackers?'

'You have eaten them yourself,' replied Ginger.

Ginger and Pickles retired into the back parlour.

They did accounts. They added up sums and sums, and sums.

'Samuel Whiskers has run up a bill as long as his tail; he has had an ounce and three-quarters of snuff since October.'

'What is seven pounds of butter at 1/3, and a stick of sealing wax and four matches?'

'Send in all the bills again to every-body "with comp^{ts}," ' replied Ginger.

After a time they heard a noise in the shop, as if something had been pushed in at the door. They came out of the back parlour. There was an envelope lying on the counter, and a policeman writing in a note-book!

Pickles nearly had a fit, he barked and he barked and made little rushes.

'Bite him, Pickles! bite him!' spluttered Ginger behind a sugar-barrel, 'he's only a German doll!'

The policeman went on writing in his notebook; twice he put his pencil in his mouth, and once he dipped it in the treacle.

Pickles barked till he was hoarse. But still the policeman took no notice. He had bead eyes, and his helmet was sewed on with stitches.

At length on his last little rush— Pickles found that the shop was empty. The policeman had disappeared.

But the envelope remained.

'Do you think that he has gone to fetch a real live policeman? I am afraid it is a summons,' said Pickles.

'No,' replied Ginger, who had opened the envelope, 'it is the rates and taxes, £3 19 11¾.'

'This is the last straw,' said Pickles, 'let us close the shop.'

They put up the shutters, and left. But they have not removed from the neighbourhood. In fact some people wish they had gone further.

Ginger is living in the warren. I do not know what occupation he pursues; he looks stout and comfortable.

Pickles is at present a gamekeeper.

The closing of the shop caused great inconvenience. Tabitha Twitchit immediately raised the price of everything a half-penny; and she continued to refuse to give credit.

Of course there are the tradesmen's carts—the butcher, the fishman and Timothy Baker.

But a person cannot live on 'seed wigs' and sponge-cake and butter-buns—not even when the sponge-cake is as good as Timothy's!

After a time Mr. John Dormouse
and his daughter began to sell pepper-
mints and candles.

But they did not keep 'self-fitting
sixes'; and it takes five mice to carry
one seven inch candle.

Besides—the candles which they sell behave very strangely in warm weather.

And Miss Dormouse refused to take back the ends when they were brought back to her with complaints.

And when Mr. John Dormouse was complained to, he stayed in bed, and would say nothing but 'very snug;' which is not the way to carry on a retail business.

So everybody was pleased when Sally Henny Penny sent out a printed poster to say that she was going to re-open the shop—'Henny's Opening Sale! Grand co-operative Jumble! Penny's penny prices! Come buy, come try, come buy!'

The poster really was most 'ticing.

There was a rush upon the opening day. The shop was crammed with customers, and there were crowds of mice upon the biscuit canisters.

Sally Henny Penny gets rather flustered when she tries to count out change, and she insists on being paid cash; but she is quite harmless.

And she has laid in a remarkable assortment of bargains.

There is something to please everybody.

DATE DUE
